Norma Lee I Don't Knock on Doors

Knock, Knock Jokes

Norma Lee I Don't Knock on Doors

Knock, Knock Jokes

compiled by Charles Keller

illustrated by Paul Galdone

Prentice-Hall, Inc.
Englewood Cliffs, New Jersey

Printed in the United States of America   ·J
Prentice-Hall International, Inc., London
Prentice-Hall of Australia, Pty. Ltd., Sydney
Prentice-Hall Canada, Inc., Toronto
Prentice-Hall of India Private Ltd., New Delhi
Prentice-Hall of Japan, Inc., Tokyo
Prentice-Hall of Southeast Asia Pte. Ltd., Singapore
Whitehall Books Limited, Wellington, New Zealand
Editora Prentice-Hall Do Brasil LTDA., Rio de Janeiro

10 9 8 7 6 5 4 3 2 1

Library of Congress Cataloging in Publication Data
Keller, Charles.
Norma Lee I don't knock on doors.
Summary: A collection of knock-knock jokes such as,
"Knock Knock.   Who's there? Europe.   Europe who? Europe
to no good."
1. Knock-knock jokes.   2. Wit and humor, Juvenile.
[1. Knock-knock jokes.   2. Jokes]   I. Galdone, Paul, ill.   II. Title.
PN6231.K55K44   1983   818′.5402   82-21549
ISBN 0-13-623587-5

Knock, knock. *Who's there?*
Norma Lee. *Norma Lee who?*
Norma Lee I don't knock on doors.

Knock, knock. *Who's there?*
Vera. *Vera who?*
Vera interesting.

Knock, knock. *Who's there?*
Snowman. *Snowman who?*
Snowman, it's a lady.

Knock, knock. *Who's there?*
Freighter. *Freighter who?*
Freighter open the door?

Knock, knock. *Who's there?*
Oliver. *Oliver who?*
Oliver troubles will be over when you open this door.

Knock, knock. *Who's there?*
Anita. *Anita who?*
Anita quarter to play a video game.

Knock, knock. *Who's there?*
Fire engine. *Fire engine who?*
Fire engine one and prepare for blast-off.

Knock, knock. *Who's there?*
Alfred. *Alfred who?*
Alfred the needle if you sew on the button.

Knock, knock. *Who's there?*
Pasture. *Pasture who?*
Pasture bedtime, isn't it?

Knock, knock. *Who's there?*
Felix. *Felix who?*
Felix cited.

Knock, knock. *Who's there?*
Westward. *Westward who?*
No, it's "Westward, ho!"

Knock, knock. *Who's there?*
Ollie. *Ollie who?*
Ollie to bed, Ollie to rise.

Knock, knock. *Who's there?*
Champ. *Champ who?*
I just did—I can't do a thing with my hair!

Knock, knock. *Who's there?*
Howie. *Howie who?*
I'm fine, how are you?

Knock, knock. *Who's there?*
Dolores. *Dolores who?*
Dolores on the side of the good guys.

Knock, knock. *Who's there?*
Boo. *Boo who?*
Don't cry, it's only a joke.

Knock, knock. *Who's there?*
Karen. *Karen who.*
Karen nuff to let me in out of the cold?

Knock, knock. *Who's there?*
Mandy. *Mandy who?*
Mandy lifeboats! De ship is sinking!

Knock, knock. *Who's there?*
Kleenex. *Kleenex who?*
Kleenex are prettier than dirty ones.

Knock, knock. *Who's there?*
Razor. *Razor who?*
Razor hands! This is a stickup.

Knock, knock. *Who's there?*
Nuisance. *Nuisance who?*
What's nuisance yesterday?

Knock, knock. *Who's there?*
Ice pick. *Ice pick who?*
Ice pick for the people of this country.

Knock, knock. *Who's there?*
Major. *Major who?*
Major answer the door, didn't I?

Knock, knock. *Who's there?*
Lettuce. *Lettuce who?*
Lettuce in and you'll find out.

Knock, knock. *Who's there?*
Zoom. *Zoom who?*
Zoom did you expect?

Knock, knock. *Who's there?*
Cargo. *Cargo who?*
Cargo beep, beep.

Knock, knock. *Who's there?*
Punch. *Punch who?*
Not me! I didn't do anything wrong.

Knock, knock. *Who's there?*
Datsun. *Datsun who?*
Datsun old joke.

Knock, knock. *Who's there?*
Moscow. *Moscow who?*
Moscow gives more milk than Pa's cow.

Knock, knock. *Who's there?*
Willis. *Willis who?*
Willis rain ever stop?

Knock, knock. *Who's there?*
Emerson. *Emerson who?*
Emerson nice shoes you got on.

Knock, knock. *Who's there?*
Premium gasoline—no knock, knock.

Knock, knock. *Who's there?*
Beef. *Beef who?*
Beef-fore I tell you, let me in.

Knock, knock. *Who's there?*
Columbus. *Columbus who?*
You Col-um-bus. I call um taxi.

Knock, knock. *Who's there?*
Junior. *Junior who?*
Junior flowers will come up.

Knock, knock. *Who's there?*
Swarm. *Swarm who?*
Swarm in the summer and cold in the winter.

Knock, knock. *Who's there?*
Kenya. *Kenya who?*
Kenya go to the movies with me?

Knock, knock. *Who's there?*
Minerva. *Minerva who?*
Minerva's wreck from all these knock, knock jokes.

Knock, knock. *Who's there?*
Honeybee. *Honeybee who?*
Honeybee nice and open the door.

Knock, knock. *Who's there?*
Cello. *Cello who?*
Cello acquaintance be forgot?

Knock, knock. *Who's there?*
Kitcheek, kitcheek. *Kitcheek, kitcheek who?*
Don't do that, I'm ticklish.

Knock, knock. *Who's there?*
Yukon. *Yukon who?*
Yukon have it. I don't want it.

Knock, knock. *Who's there?*
Ella. *Ella who?*
Ella-mentary, my dear Watson.

Knock, knock. *Who's there?*
Eiffel. *Eiffel who?*
Eiffel down and hurt myself.

Knock, knock. *Who's there?*
Annapolis. *Annapolis who?*
Annapolis a fruit.

Knock, knock. *Who's there?*
Howell. *Howell who?*
Howell you have your hamburger, medium or well done?

Knock, knock. *Who's there?*
Europe. *Europe who?*
Europe to no good.

Knock, knock. *Who's there?*
Hank. *Hank who?*
You're welcome.

Knock, knock. *Who's there?*
Arkansas. *Arkansas who?*
Arkansas more wood with my new chain saw.

Knock, knock. *Who's there?*
Madison. *Madison who?*
Madison the doctor gave me cured my cough.

Knock, knock. *Who's there?*
Tinker Bell. *Tinker Bell who?*
Tinker Bell is out of order.

Knock, knock. *Who's there?*
Toyota. *Toyota who?*
Toyota be a law against knock, knock jokes!

Knock, knock. *Who's there?*
Could she. *Could she who?*
Could she, could she coo.

Knock, knock. *Who's there?*
Lion. *Lion who?*
Lion down on the job again?

Knock, knock. *Who's there?*
Ivan. *Ivan who?*
Ivan itch where I can't scratch.

Knock, knock. *Who's there?*
Lilac. *Lilac who?*
Lilac that and you'll get punished!

Knock, knock. *Who's there?*
Omar. *Omar who?*
Omar goodness! Wrong address.

Knock, knock. *Who's there?*
Freddy. *Freddy who?*
Freddy or not, here I come.

Knock, knock. *Who's there?*
Osborn. *Osborn who?*
Osborn in the state of California.

Knock, knock. *Who's there?*
Earl. *Earl who?*
Earl I want for Christmas is my two front teeth.

Knock, knock. *Who's there?*
Sofa. *Sofa who?*
Sofa, so good.

Knock, knock. *Who's there?*
Howard Hughes. *Howard Hughes who?*
Howard Hughes like a piece of candy?

Knock, knock. *Who's there?*
Amnesia. *Amnesia who?*
Oh, you've got it, too.

Knock, knock. *Who's there?*
Banana. *Banana who?*
Knock, knock. *Who's there?*
Banana. *Banana who?*
Knock, knock. *Who's there?*
Orange. *Orange who?*
Orange you glad it's not another banana?

Knock, knock. *Who's there?*
Tuna. *Tuna who?*
Tuna radio down. It's making too much noise.

Knock, knock. *Who's there?*
Argo. *Argo who?*
Argo chase yourself.

Knock, knock. *Who's there?*
Linda. *Linda who?*
Linda helping hand.

Knock, knock. *Who's there?*
Freeze. *Freeze who?*
Freeze a jolly good fellow.

Knock, knock. *Who's there?*
Window. *Window who?*
Window we eat?

Knock, knock. *Who's there?*
Butter. *Butter who?*
Butter open up before I melt.

Knock, knock. *Who's there?*
Value. *Value who?*
Value be my Valentine?

Knock, knock. *Who's there?*
Cairo. *Cairo who?*
Cairo the boat now?

Knock, knock. *Who's there?*
Closure. *Closure who?*
Closure mouth and open the door.

Knock, knock. *Who's there?*
Max. *Max who?*
Max no difference.

Knock, knock. *Who's there?*
Oliver. *Oliver who?*
Oliver the world people are telling knock, knock
jokes.

Knock, knock. *Who's there?*
Fortification. *Fortification who?*
Fortification I go to the beach.

Knock, knock. *Who's there?*
Mickey. *Mickey who?*
Mickey's stuck in the lock and I can't get in.

Knock, knock. *Who's there?*
Avenue. *Avenue who?*
Avenue baby sister.

Knock, knock. *Who's there?*
Juicy. *Juicy who?*
Juicy that bird fly over?

Knock, knock. *Who's there?*
Venice. *Venice who?*
Venice lunch?

Knock, knock. *Who's there?*
Lena. *Lena who?*
Lena little closer and I'll tell you.

Knock, knock. *Who's there?*
Cash. *Cash who?*
Are you some kind of nut?

Knock, knock. *Who's there?*
Saul. *Saul who?*
Saul the king's horses and Saul the king's men.

Knock, knock. *Who's there?*
Eileen. *Eileen who?*
Eileen down to tie my shoes.

Knock, knock. *Who's there?*
A.E. *A.E. who?*
A.E. I owe you.

Knock, knock. *Who's there?*
Cantaloupe. *Cantaloupe who?*
Cantaloupe tonight. Dad has the car.

Knock, knock. *Who's there?*
Welfare. *Welfare who?*
Welfare crying out loud!

Knock, knock. *Who's there?*
Amy Namath. *Amy Namath who?*
Amy Namath Alice and my husband's name is Allen.

Knock, knock. *Who's there?*
Havana. *Havana who?*
Havana wonderful time, wish you were here!

Knock, knock. *Who's there?*
Stopwatch. *Stopwatch who?*
Stopwatch you're doing.

Knock, knock. *Who's there?*
Sue. *Sue who?*
Don't ask me. I'm not your lawyer.

Knock, knock. *Who's there?*
Franz. *Franz who?*
Franz, Romans, countrymen.

Knock, knock. *Who's there?*
Cereal. *Cereal who?*
Cereal pleasure to meet you.

Knock, knock. *Who's there?*
Tank. *Tank who?*
You're welcome.
Knock, knock. *Who's there?*
Dimension. *Dimension who?*
Dimension it.

Knock, knock. *Who's there?*
A person who is too short to reach the doorbell.

Knock, knock. *Who's there?*
Snow. *Snow who?*
Snow doubt about it, you need a haircut.

Knock, knock. *Who's there?*
Mary Lee. *Mary Lee who?*
Mary Lee we roll along.

Knock, knock. *Who's there?*
Toby. *Toby who?*
Toby, or not Toby: that is the question.

Knock, knock. *Who's there?*
Ice cream soda. *Ice cream soda who?*
Ice cream soda whole world will hear me.

Knock, knock. *Who's there?*
Dick. *Dick who?*
Dick 'em up! I'm a tongue-tied wobber.

Knock, knock. *Who's there?*
Honeydew. *Honeydew who?*
Honeydew you love me?

Knock, knock. *Who's there?*
Henrietta and Juliet. *Henrietta and Juliet who?*
Henrietta big dinner and got sick. Juliet the same
thing, but she's okay.

Knock, knock. *Who's there?*
Arthur. *Arthur who?*
Arthur any more at home like you?

Knock, knock. *Who's there?*
Hector. *Hector who?*
Hector halls with boughs of holly.

Knock, knock. *Who's there?*
Gorilla. *Gorilla who?*
Gorilla my dreams, I love you.

Knock, knock. *Who's there?*
Hoover. *Hoover who?*
Hoover you expecting?

Knock, knock. *Who's there?*
Winnie. *Winnie who?*
Winnie you going to think up a better joke?

Knock, knock. *Who's there?*
Warrior. *Warrior who?*
Warrior been all my life?

Knock, knock. *Who's there?*
X. *X who?*
X for breakfast.

Knock, knock. *Who's there?*
Acme. *Acme who?*
Acme in and you'll find out.

Knock, knock. *Who's there?*
O'Shea. *O'Shea who?*
O'Shea, can you see?

Knock, knock. *Who's there?*
Maybelle. *Maybelle who?*
Maybelle doesn't ring either.

Knock, knock. *Who's there?*
Orange juice. *Orange juice who?*
Orange juice sorry you made me cry?

Knock, knock. *Who's there?*
Pickle. *Pickle who?*
Pickle number from 1 to 10.

Knock, knock. *Who's there?*
Thumping. *Thumping who?*
Thumping green and slimy is climbing up your neck.

Knock, knock. *Who's there?*
Disguise. *Disguise who?*
Disguise the limit!

Knock, knock. *Who's there?*
Gladys. *Gladys who?*
Gladys Friday, aren't you?

Knock, knock. *Who's there?*
Jamaica. *Jamaica who?*
Jamaica passing grade in the math test?

Knock, knock. *Who's there?*
Wooden shoe. *Wooden shoe who?*
Wooden shoe like to know?

Knock, knock. *Who's there?*
Arizona. *Arizona who?*
Arizona room for one of us in this town, so you'd
better get on your horse and ride.

Knock, knock. *Who's there?*
Spectator. *Spectator who?*
Do you spectators will grow good this year?

Knock, knock. *Who's there?*
Eyes. *Eyes who?*
Eyes got another knock, knock joke.
Knock, knock. *Who's there?*
Nose. *Nose who?*
I nose another knock, knock joke.
Knock, knock. *Who's there?*
Ears. *Ears who?*
Ears another knock, knock joke.
Knock, knock. *Who's there?*
Chin. *Chin who?*
Chin up, I'm not going to tell another knock, knock
joke.